The MAGIC FISH-BONE

Illustrated by

ROBERT FLORCZAK

The Rainbow Bridge
by Audrey Wood

Rough Sketch Beginning
by James Berry

Birdsong
by Audrey Wood

The Persian Cinderella
by Shirley Climo

The MAGIC FISH-BONE

Romance. From the pen of Miss Alice Rainbird. (Aged seven.)

CHARLES DICKENS

with pictures in color by

ROBERT FLORCZAK

HARCOURT, INC. • San Diego New York London

"The Magic Fish-bone" was originally published in the January–May issue of *Our Young Folks* in 1868,
and in 1883 was collected in the book *A Child's History of England,* in a section entitled "Holiday Romance."

www.harcourt.com

Library of Congress Cataloging-in-Publication Data
Dickens, Charles, 1812–1870.
The magic fish-bone/Charles Dickens; illustrated by Robert Florczak.
p. cm.
Summary: King Watkins the First is proud of his eldest daughter's magical gift but wonders why she isn't using it.
[1. Fairy tales.] I. Florczak, Robert, ill. II. Title.
PZ8.D6 2000
[Fic]—dc21 96-53972
ISBN 0-15-201080-7

First edition
Printed in Hong Kong

A C E G H F D B

Some terms from Dickens's time will be unfamiliar to modern readers.
To be under government *meant to work for the government, to be a civil servant.*
In Victorian times, civil servants were paid once every three months—that is, once every quarter—
on what was known as quarter-day. *As to why a* king *and* queen *would have to wait*
for quarter-day pay…the reader should remember that in Victorian times, as today,
a child's parents were always and ever no less than royalty.

For my little ones,
Lily and Lukas

——R. F.

THERE WAS ONCE A KING, and he had a queen; and he was the manliest of his sex, and she was the loveliest of hers. The king was, in his private profession, under government. The queen's father had been a medical man out of town.

They had nineteen children and were always having more. Seventeen of these children took care of the baby; and Alicia, the eldest, took care of them all. Their ages varied from seven years to seven months.

Let us now resume our story.

One day the king was going to the office when he stopped at the fishmonger's to buy a pound and a half of salmon not too near the tail, which the queen (who was a careful housekeeper) had requested him to send home.

Mr. Pickles, the fishmonger, said, "Certainly, sir. Is there any other article? Good morning."

The king went on towards the office in a melancholy mood, for quarter-day was such a long way off, and several of the dear children were growing out of their clothes. He had not proceeded far when Mr. Pickles's errand boy came running after him

and said, "Sir, you didn't notice the old lady in our shop."

"What old lady?" inquired the king. "I saw none."

Now the king had not seen any old lady, because this old lady had been invisible to him, though visible to Mr. Pickles's boy. Probably because the boy messed and splashed the water about to such a degree, and flopped the pairs of soles down in such a violent manner, that if she had not been visible to him, he would have spoilt her clothes.

Just then the old lady came trotting up. She was dressed in shot-silk of the richest quality, smelling of dried lavender.

"King Watkins the First, I believe," said the old lady.

"Watkins," replied the king, "is my name."

"Papa, if I am not mistaken, of the beautiful Princess Alicia?" said the old lady.

"And of eighteen other darlings," replied the king.

"Listen. You are going to the office," said the old lady.

It instantly flashed upon the king that she must be a fairy, or how could she know that?

"You are right," said the old lady, answering his thoughts. "I am the good Fairy Grandmarina. Attend! When you return home to dinner, politely invite the Princess Alicia to have some of the salmon you bought just now."

"It may disagree with her," said the king.

The old lady became so very angry at this absurd idea that the king was quite alarmed and humbly begged her pardon.

"We hear a great deal too much about this thing disagreeing and that thing disagreeing," said the old lady, with the greatest

contempt it was possible to express. "Don't be greedy. I think you want it all for yourself."

The king hung his head under this reproof and said he wouldn't talk about things disagreeing anymore.

"Be good, then," said the Fairy Grandmarina, "and don't. When the beautiful Princess Alicia consents to partake of the salmon—as I think she will—you will find she will leave a fishbone on her plate. Tell her to dry it, and to rub it, and to polish it till it shines like mother-of-pearl, and to take care of it as a present from me."

"Is that all?" asked the king.

"Don't be impatient, sir," returned the Fairy Grandmarina, scolding him severely. "Don't catch people short, before they have done speaking. Just the way with you grown-up persons. You are always doing it."

The king again hung his head and said he wouldn't do so anymore.

"Be good, then," said the Fairy Grandmarina, "and don't! Tell the Princess Alicia, with my love, that the fish-bone is a magic present which can only be used once; but that it will bring her, that once, whatever she wishes for, *provided she wishes for it at the right time*. That is the message. Take care of it."

The king was beginning, "Might I ask the reason?" when the fairy became absolutely furious.

"*Will* you be good, sir?" she exclaimed, stamping her foot on the ground. "The reason for this and the reason for that, indeed! You are always wanting the reason. No reason. There! Hoity-toity me! I am sick of your grown-up reasons."

The king was extremely frightened by the old lady's flying into such a passion and said he was very sorry to have offended her and he wouldn't ask for reasons anymore.

"Be good, then," said the old lady, "and don't."

With these words Grandmarina vanished, and the king went on and on and on, till he came to the office. There he wrote and wrote and wrote, till it was time to go home again. Then he politely invited the Princess Alicia, as the fairy had directed him, to partake of the salmon. And when she had enjoyed it very much, he saw the fish-bone on her plate, as the fairy had told him he would, and he delivered the fairy's message, and the Princess Alicia took care to dry the bone, and to rub it, and to polish it till it shone like mother-of-pearl.

And so, when the queen was going to get up in the morning, she said, "Oh, dear me, dear me. My head, my head!" and then she fainted away.

The Princess Alicia, who happened to be looking in at the chamber door, asking about breakfast, was very much alarmed when she saw her royal mamma in this state, and she rang the bell for Peggy, which was the name of the lord chamberlain. But remembering where the smelling bottle was, she climbed on a chair and got it; and after that she climbed on another chair by the bedside and held the smelling bottle to the queen's nose; and after that she jumped down and got some water; and after that she jumped up again and wetted the queen's forehead; and in short, when the lord chamberlain came in, that dear old woman said to the little princess, "What a trot you are! I couldn't have done it better myself!"

But that was not the worst of the good queen's illness. Oh no! She was very ill indeed for a long time. The Princess

Alicia kept the seventeen young princes and princesses quiet, and dressed and undressed and danced the baby, and made the kettle boil, and heated the soup, and swept the hearth, and poured out the medicine, and nursed the queen, and did all that ever she could, and was as busy, busy, busy as busy could be; for there were not many servants at that palace, for three reasons: because the king was short of money, because a rise in his office never seemed to come, and because quarter-day was so far off that it looked almost as far off and as little as one of the stars.

But on the morning when the queen fainted away, where was the magic fish-bone? Why there it was in Princess Alicia's pocket! She had almost taken it out to bring the queen to life again, when she put it back and looked for the smelling bottle.

After the queen had come out of her swoon that morning and was dozing, the Princess Alicia hurried upstairs to tell a most particular secret to a most particularly confidential friend of hers, who was a duchess, though nobody knew it except the princess.

This most particular secret was the secret about the magic fish-bone, the history of which was well known to the duchess, because the princess told her everything. The princess kneeled down by the bed on which the duchess was lying, full dressed and wide awake, and whispered the secret to her. The duchess smiled and nodded. People might have supposed that she never smiled and nodded; but she often did, though nobody knew it except the princess.

Then the Princess Alicia hurried downstairs again, to keep
watch in the queen's room. She often kept watch by herself in the
queen's room; but every evening while the illness lasted she sat
there watching with the king. And every evening the king sat

looking at her with a cross look, wondering why she never brought out the magic fish-bone. As often as she noticed this, she ran upstairs, whispered the secret to the duchess over again, and said to the duchess besides, "They think we children never have a reason or a meaning!" And the duchess, though the most fashionable duchess that ever was heard of, winked her eye.

"Alicia," said the king one evening, when she wished him good night.

"Yes, Papa."

"What is become of the magic fish-bone?"

"In my pocket, Papa."

"I thought you had lost it?"

"Oh no, Papa!"

"Or forgotten it?"

"No, indeed, Papa."

And so another time the dreadful little snapping pug-dog next door made a rush at one of the young princes as he stood on the steps coming home from school, and terrified him out of his wits, and he put his hand through a pane of glass and bled, bled, bled. When the seventeen other young princes and princesses saw him bleed, bleed, bleed, they were terrified out of their wits, too, and screamed themselves black in their seventeen faces all at once. But the Princess Alicia put her hands over all their seventeen mouths, one after another, and persuaded them to be quiet because of the sick queen.

And then she put the wounded prince's hand in a basin of fresh cold water while they stared with their twice-seventeen-are-thirty-four, put-down-four-and-carry-three eyes, and then she looked in the hand for bits of glass, and there were fortunately no bits of glass there. And then she said to two chubby-legged princes, who were sturdy, though small, "Bring me in the royal ragbag: I must snip and stitch and cut and contrive." So these two young princes tugged at the royal ragbag and lugged it in; and the Princess Alicia sat down on the floor with a large pair of scissors and a needle and thread, and snipped and stitched, and cut and contrived, and made a bandage, and put it on, and it fitted beautifully; and so, when it was all done, she saw the king, her papa, looking on by the door.

"Alicia."

"Yes, Papa."

"What have you been doing?"

"Snipping, stitching, cutting, and contriving, Papa."

"Where is the magic fish-bone?"

"In my pocket, Papa!"

"I thought you had lost it?"

"Oh no, Papa!"

"Or forgotten it?"

"No, indeed, Papa."

After that, she ran upstairs to the duchess, and told her what had passed, and told her the secret over again; and the duchess shook her flaxen curls and laughed with her rosy lips.

Well! And so another time the baby fell under the grate. The seventeen young princes and princesses were used to it, for they were almost always falling under the grate or down the stairs; but the baby was not used to it yet, and it gave him a swelled face and a black eye. The way the poor little darling came to tumble was that he was out of the Princess Alicia's lap just as she was sitting, in a great coarse apron that quite smothered her, in front of the kitchen fire, beginning to peel the turnips for the broth for dinner; and the way she came to be doing that was that the king's cook had run away that morning with her own true love, who was a very tall but very tipsy soldier. Then the seventeen young princes and princesses, who cried at everything that happened, cried and roared. But the Princess Alicia (who couldn't help crying a little herself) quietly called to them to be still, on account of not throwing back the queen upstairs, who was fast getting well, and said, "Hold your tongues, you wicked little monkeys, every one of you, while I examine Baby!"

Then she examined the baby and found that he hadn't broken anything; and she held cold iron to his poor dear eye and smoothed his poor dear face, and he presently fell asleep in her arms. Then she said to the seventeen princes and princesses, "I am afraid to let him down yet, lest he should wake and feel pain; be good and you shall all be cooks."

They jumped for joy when they heard that and began making themselves cooks' caps out of old newspapers. So to one she gave the salt box, and to one she gave the barley, and to one she gave the herbs, and to one she gave the turnips, and to one she gave the carrots, and to one she gave the onions, and to one she gave the spice box, till they were all cooks and all running about at work, she sitting in the middle, smothered in the great coarse apron, nursing baby. By and by the broth was done; and the baby woke up, smiling like an angel, and was trusted to the sedatest princess to hold, while the other princes and princesses were squeezed into a far-off corner to look at the Princess Alicia turning out the saucepanful of broth, for fear (as they were always getting into trouble) they should get splashed and scalded. When the broth came tumbling out, steaming beautifully and smelling like a nosegay good to eat, they clapped their hands. That made the baby clap his hands; and that, and his looking as if he had a comic

toothache, made all the princes and princesses laugh. So the Princess Alicia said, "Laugh and be good; and after dinner we will make him a nest on the floor in a corner, and he shall sit in his nest and see a dance of eighteen cooks."

That delighted the young princes and princesses, and they ate up all the broth, and washed up all the plates and dishes, and cleared away, and pushed the table into a corner; and then they in their cooks' caps, and the Princess Alicia in the smothering coarse apron that belonged to the cook that had run away with her own true love that was the very tall but very tipsy soldier, danced a dance of eighteen cooks before the angelic baby, who forgot his swelled face and his black eye and crowed with joy.

And so then once more the Princess Alicia saw King Watkins the First, her father, standing in the doorway looking on, and he said, "What have you been doing, Alicia?"

"Cooking and contriving, Papa."

"What else have you been doing, Alicia?"

"Keeping the children lighthearted, Papa."

"Where is the magic fish-bone, Alicia?"

"In my pocket, Papa."

"I thought you had lost it?"

"Oh no, Papa!"

"Or forgotten it?"

"No, indeed, Papa."

The king then sighed so heavily, and seemed so low-spirited, and sat down so miserably, leaning his head upon his hand and his elbow upon the kitchen table pushed away in the corner, that the seventeen princes and princesses crept softly out of the kitchen and left him alone with the Princess Alicia and the angelic baby.

"What is the matter, Papa?"

"I am dreadfully poor, my child."

"Have you no money at all, Papa?"

"None, my child."

"Is there no way of getting any, Papa?"

"No way," said the king. "I have tried very hard, and I have tried all ways."

When she heard those last words, the Princess Alicia began to put her hand into the pocket where she kept the magic fish-bone.

"Papa," said she, "when we have tried very hard, and tried all ways, we must have done our very, very best?"

"No doubt, Alicia."

"When we have done our very, very best, Papa, and that is not enough, then I think the right time must have come for asking help of others." This was the very secret connected with the magic fish-bone, which she had found out for herself from the good Fairy Grandmarina's words, and which she had so often whispered to her beautiful and fashionable friend, the duchess.

So she took out of her pocket the magic fish-bone, which had been dried and rubbed and polished till it shone like mother-of-pearl; and she gave it one little kiss and wished it was quarter-day. And immediately it *was* quarter-day, and the king's quarter's salary came rattling down the chimney and bounced into the middle of the floor.

But this was not half of what happened—no, not a quarter—for immediately afterwards the good Fairy Grandmarina came riding in, in a carriage and four (peacocks), with Mr. Pickles's boy up behind, dressed in silver and gold, with a cocked hat, powdered hair, pink silk stockings, a jeweled cane, and a nosegay.

Down jumped Mr. Pickles's boy, with his cocked hat in his hand and wonderfully polite (being entirely changed by enchantment), and handed Grandmarina out; and there she stood in her rich shot-silk smelling of dried lavender, fanning herself with a sparkling fan.

"Alicia, my dear," said this charming old fairy, "how do you do? I hope I see you pretty well? Give me a kiss."

The Princess Alicia embraced her, and then Grandmarina turned to the king and said rather sharply, "Are you good?"

The king said he hoped so.

"I suppose you know the reason *now* why my goddaughter here"—kissing the princess again—"did not apply to the fish-bone sooner?" said the fairy.

The king made a shy bow.

"Ah! But you didn't *then*?" said the fairy.

The king made a shyer bow.

"Any more reasons to ask for?" said the fairy.

The king said, No, and he was very sorry.

"Be good, then," said the fairy, "and live happily ever afterwards."

Then Grandmarina waved her fan, and the queen came in most splendidly dressed; and the seventeen young princes and princesses, no longer grown out of their clothes, came in, newly fitted out from top to toe, with tucks in everything to admit of its being let out. After that, the fairy tapped the Princess Alicia with her fan; and the smothering coarse apron flew away, and she appeared exquisitely dressed, like a little bride, with a wreath of orange flowers and a silver veil. After that, the kitchen dresser changed of itself into a wardrobe made of beautiful woods and gold and looking-glass, which was full of dresses of all sorts, all for her and all exactly fitting her. After that, the angelic baby came in, running alone, with his face and eye not a bit the worse, but much the better. Then Grandmarina begged to be introduced to the duchess, and when the duchess was brought down, many compliments passed between them.

A little whispering took place between the fairy and the duchess, and then the fairy said out aloud, "Yes, I thought she would have told you." Grandmarina then turned to the king and queen and said, "We are going in search of Prince Certainpersonio. The pleasure of your company is requested at church in half an hour precisely." So she and the Princess Alicia got into the carriage; and Mr. Pickles's boy handed in the duchess, who sat by herself on the opposite seat; and then Mr. Pickles's boy put up the steps and got up behind, and the peacocks flew away with their tails behind.

Prince Certainpersonio was sitting by himself, eating barley sugar, and waiting to be ninety. When he saw the peacocks, followed by the carriage, coming in at the window, it immediately occurred to him that something uncommon was going to happen.

"Prince," said Grandmarina, "I bring you your bride."

The moment the fairy said those words, Prince Certainpersonio's face left off being sticky, and his jacket and corduroys
changed to peach-bloom velvet, and his hair curled, and a cap
and feather flew in like a bird and settled on his head. He got
into the carriage by the fairy's invitation; and there he renewed
his acquaintance with the duchess, whom he had seen before.

In the church were the prince's relations and friends, and the
Princess Alicia's relations and friends, and the seventeen princes
and princesses, and the baby, and a crowd of the neighbors. The
marriage was beautiful beyond expression. The duchess was
bridesmaid and beheld the ceremony from the pulpit, where she
was supported by the cushion of the desk.

Grandmarina gave a magnificent wedding feast afterwards, in which there was everything and more to eat, and everything and more to drink. The wedding cake was delicately ornamented with white satin ribbons, frosted silver, and white lilies, and was forty-two yards round.

When Grandmarina had drunk her love to the young couple, and Prince Certainpersonio had made a speech, and everybody had cried, "Hip, hip, hip, hurrah!" Grandmarina announced to the king and queen that in future there would be eight quarter-days in every year, except in leap year, when there would be ten. She then turned to Certainpersonio and Alicia and said, "My dears, you will have thirty-five children, and they will all be good and beautiful. Seventeen of your children will be boys, and eighteen will be girls. The hair of the whole of your children will curl naturally. They will never have the measles and will have recovered from the whooping cough before being born."

On hearing such good news, everybody cried out, "Hip, hip, hip, hurrah!" again.

"It only remains," said Grandmarina in conclusion, "to make an end of the fish-bone."

So she took it from the hand of Princess Alicia, and it instantly flew down the throat of the dreadful little snapping pug-dog next door and choked him, and he expired in convulsions.

The illustrations in this book were done in French Grey pencil and oil on paper.

The display type was based on an alphabet designed by Charles Robinson.

The text type was set in Granjon.

Printed by South China Printing Company, Ltd., Hong Kong

This book was printed on totally chlorine-free Nymolla Matte Art paper.

Production supervision by Ginger Boyer

Designed by Linda Lockowitz and Michael Farmer